Dinosaurs!

The biggest
baddest
strangest
fastest

Dinosaurs!

The biggest baddest strangest fastest

by Howard Zimmerman

GEORGE OLSHEVSKY
SCIENCE CONSULTANT

A BYRON PREISS VISUAL PUBLICATIONS, INC. BOOK

ATHENEUM BOOKS FOR YOUNG READERS
NEW YORK · LONDON · TORONTO · SYDNEY · SINGAPORE

ACKNOWLEDGMENTS

Many thanks to the paleo-art community for making this book a special collection of wonderful illustrations, and in particular to Mike Fredericks for sending out the call. A special thanks to Caitlyn Dlouhy who went above and beyond the call of duty to ensure that this book would be special.

DEDICATION

This book is dedicated to Charles Knight and Rudolph Zalinger for creating the soaring visions that captured my heart and imagination as a child, to my father for insisting that dinosaurs were real, and to my mother for teaching me how to read. —H.Z.

ART CREDITS

Page 1: A group of Cretaceous creatures by Alex Ebel
Page 2: A group of Antarctic dinosaurs by William Stout
Page 7: A rearing Chasmosaurus by Gregory Paul
Pages 8 and 9: Various dinosaur groups by John Sibbick

Atheneum Books for Young Readers
An imprint of Simon & Schuster
Children's Publishing Division
1230 Avenue of the Americas
New York, New York 10020

The text of this book is set in Cheltenham.
Interior design by Gilda Hannah
Printed in Hong Kong

4   6   8   10   9   7   5

Library of Congress Cataloging-in-Publication Data
Zimmerman, Howard.
Dinosaurs! the biggest baddest strangest fastest /
by Howard Zimmerman.   p. cm.
Summary: Present facts about and illustrations of dinosaurs,
grouped by size, speed, eating habits, and appearance.
ISBN 0-689-83276-1 (alk. paper)
1. Dinosaurs—Juvenile literature. [1. Dinosaurs.] I. Title.
QE862.D5 .Z53 2000   567.9—dc21   99-42464

CONTENTS

Dinosaurs!

The biggest
baddest
strangest
fastest

INTRODUCTION

The names alone are enough to send your blood rushing: *Velociraptor, Seismosaurus, Tyrannosaurus rex*. Dinosaurs. They came in all sizes and a vast variety of shapes. They were the ancient monsters of our planet's dim past.

The dinosaurs were the largest, strangest group of animals ever to walk the Earth. They were also one of the most successful. Although the last dinosaurs died about 65 million years ago, the dinosaur families ruled the planet for more than 160 million years. Modern humans and the family of animals of which people are a part have only been around for about 2 to 3 million years.

Although the dinosaurs are long gone, the science that investigates them is alive and well. Discoveries of new dinosaurs happen more often than you would think. In fact, there have been more new dinosaurs discovered in the past 10 years than in the 50 years before that. Not only are new dinosaurs being dug up, scientists are finding out more about them all the time.

Triassic dinosaurs

There are several ways of grouping the dinosaurs. One way is by the time during which they lived. Dinosaurs ruled the Earth during three different time periods:

The Triassic Period—245 Million Years Ago to 205 Million Years Ago
The Jurassic Period—205 Million Years Ago to 140 Million Years Ago
The Cretaceous Period—140 Million Years Ago to 65 Million Years Ago

Together, these three time periods make up what is called the Mesozoic (mess-uh-ZO-ic) Era.

Scientists have also divided dinosaurs into two major groups based on part of their bone structure. The two groups are saurischian (saw-RISS-key-in) dinosaurs and ornithischian (or-ni-THISS-key-in) dinosaurs. Saurischian means "lizard hipped." Ornithischian means "bird hipped." Every dinosaur that ever lived was either lizard hipped or bird hipped. And both groups existed throughout all three time periods of the Mesozoic Era.

The ornithischians were mostly four-legged plant eaters. They were the mid-sized to smaller plant eaters, relatively speaking. They include dinosaurs that were armored, dinosaurs with spikes and horns, and the duck-billed dinosaurs. *Ankylosaurus* and *Stegosaurus* were the most massive of the four-legged ornithischians. Duck-billed dinosaurs and *Iguanodons* probably ran on two legs but walked on all fours. They were also ornithischian dinosaurs.

The saurischian dinosaurs are divided into two sub-groups. These are the theropods and the sauropods. The sauropods were the huge, four-legged plant eaters, like *Seismosaurus* and *Brachiosaurus*. They were the biggest animals ever to roam the planet. The theropods were the two-legged meat eaters, like *Allosaurus* and *Tyrannosaurus*. They were deadly hunters and scavengers.

Jurassic dinosaurs

For this book, we have chosen another way of dividing the dinosaurs. We have grouped them according to their size and speed, their eating habits and how they looked. And we'll also tell you when and where they lived, and what kind of dinosaurs they were.

No one knows *exactly* how the dinosaurs looked when they were alive. But many scientists think that they could see colors, like birds do today. Animals that see in color often have bright coloring themselves. Many artists paint their dinosaurs with the bright coloration of lizards and birds, which happen to be the dinosaurs' closest living relatives. Some artists have given the more bird-like dinosaurs a covering of downy feathers. The paintings in this book represent the very latest thinking on how the great beasts might have looked, but again, no one knows for sure.

Cretaceous dinosaurs

In the back of the book we'll give you a list of dinosaur Web sites that you can visit on the Internet. The sites are free, and you can visit them on your computer at home, in school, or in the library.

We hope that this is just the beginning of your dinosaur adventures. There is much more to learn about the vanished monsters of the Mesozoic. Keep following your interests. One day some of you may become dinosaur scientists, digging for buried fossils in the remote corners of the globe. And perhaps, if you're lucky, you may discover a new kind of dinosaur—one that has never been seen before. As its discoverer, you would get to name it. Imagine a dinosaur named after . . . you!

The Biggest Plant Eaters

MAMENCHISAURUS

(ma-MEN-chi-SAW-rus)

Mamenchisaurus is one of the largest dinosaurs ever discovered in Asia. Its neck alone reached a remarkable 35 feet in length, which is the longest known neck of any animal that ever lived. From head to tail, *Mamenchisaurus* was over 75 feet long.

Mamenchisaurus's long neck was quite strong. This giant could probably feed from several trees at the same time, which is a neat trick. And it probably did this while standing still. The front end of the neck was fairly flexible, allowing *Mamenchisaurus* to move its mouth left and right and up and down like a giant vacuum cleaner.

Mamenchisaurus was a member of the dinosaur group called sauropods. They were all gigantic, four-legged plant eaters. *Mamenchisaurus* means "Mamenchi lizard." It was named after the place where it was found in southern China. Its fossils have never been found anywhere else. The huge plant eater lived 155 to 145 million years ago. In 1993, a close relative to *Mamenchisaurus* was also discovered in China. It's named *Hudiesaurus* (HOO-die-eh-SAW-rus), and it may have grown even larger than *Mamenchisaurus,* as much as 90 feet long. Not enough pieces of the entire skeleton were found, however, so scientists can't be sure.

**Top: A *Mamenchisaurus* and her baby are separated from the herd.
Opposite page, middle: A pack of *Allosaurus* picks up the scent.
Opposite page, bottom: When the baby falls behind its mother,
they attack.**

BRACHIOSAURUS

(BRACK-ee-uh-SAW-rus)

Brachiosaurus was one of the longest and tallest animals that ever lived. Built like a giraffe, it was 90 to 100 feet long, and its head sat 40 feet in the air atop its long, strong neck. This dinosaur was *big*. When fully grown it weighed as much as 80 tons, which is the same as a dozen African elephants. Like *Mamenchisaurus*, *Brachiosaurus* was one of the giant plant-eating dinosaurs called sauropods.

Brachiosaurus was a four-legged dinosaur, but its front legs were longer and thinner than its hind legs. Its name refers to these rather slender limbs, and means "lizard arm." *Brachiosaurus* had large nostril openings high up on its head, between and above its eyes. Scientists aren't quite sure of their purpose, but they may have helped it to smell its favorite food. Its large teeth were shaped like chisels, perfect for cropping off leaves and branches. These enormous dinosaurs ate treetops, leaves, and branches.

Brachiosaurus lived from about 155 million years ago to about 145 million years ago. They were successful animals that roamed across the globe. Their fossils have been found in Europe, the western United States, and in East Africa.

Opposite: A giant *Brachiosaurus* moves through the forest, scaring away the prey of an angry *Ceratosaurus*. Above: A young *Stegosaurus* tries to avoid being stepped on by a *Brachiosaurus*.

13

SEISMOSAURUS

(SIZE-muh-SAW-rus)

If you name an animal "earthshaking lizard," which is what *Seismosaurus* means, it had better be pretty huge. This dinosaur wasn't just big, it is the largest dinosaur ever discovered. It was anywhere from 120 to 170 feet long, fully grown, and the ground must have shaken indeed when this monster moved.

Seismosaurus lived at the same time as *Brachiosaurus* and *Mamenchisaurus*, about 155 to 145 million years ago. It was a member of the diplodocid dinosaur family. Some scientists think it had an incredibly long, strong, whiplike tail, which it could have used to defend itself from attacking predators.

To reach such a massive size, *Seismosaurus* must have eaten tons of plants and trees every day. How did it manage to digest all of that tough wood and plant fiber? Scientists think it swallowed small rocks called gizzard stones. These would have helped crush the plants to a pulp in the dinosaur's stomach. Gizzard stones have been found with the fossils of many sauropods and other plant-eating dinosaurs. They are almost always found in the area where the animal's stomach would have been. When *Seismosaurus* was first discovered, *two* piles of gizzard stones were found with the skeleton. This suggests that the dinosaur had two different digestive organs. But this is not so unusual. Cows and other plant eaters living today have a second stomach to help digest coarse plant fiber.

So far, *Seismosaurus* fossils have only been found in the southwest of the United States. Complete leg fossils for *Seismosaurus* have yet to be found. But scientists think it must have had short, thick legs, and may have spent a lot of time wading in water to ease the strain caused by its enormous weight.

A herd of *Seismosaurus* crosses a flood plain to find fresh forests to eat.

Above: A hungry
T. rex tries to
make a meal of
a 20-foot-long
Pentaceratops.
Bottom: When
T. rex was on the
move, animals
scattered.

The Biggest Meat Eaters

TYRANNOSAURUS REX

(tie-RAN-uh-SAW-rus REX)

Tyrannosaurus rex is perhaps the best-known dinosaur in the world. This monster's name means "king tyrant lizard." A whole family of dinosaurs, called tyrannosaurids, was named after it. Tyrannosaurids were highly specialized meat eaters with small front limbs, huge heads, and powerful jaws. They were the last of the great theropods. The best-known tyrannosaurids are *Tyrannosaurus, Tarbosaurus, Gorgosaurus, Albertosaurus*, and *Daspletosaurus*. They lived from about 80 to 65 million years ago in the western United States and eastern Asia.

At 40 feet long, and weighing as much as 6 tons, *Tyrannosaurus rex* was the largest meat-eating dinosaur ever to live in North America. *Tyrannosaurus* fossils have been found from the southern state of New Mexico all the way north to western Canada.

Scientists aren't sure if *T. rex* hunted alone (opposite) or in pairs (above). But they're pretty certain that *Tyrannosaurus* scavenged on dead animals as well as hunted live ones (left).

T. rex's enormous skull was filled with 6-inch-long dagger-like teeth made for biting and tearing through flesh and bone. It had a short, stout neck, and incredibly strong jaw muscles. This dinosaur could rip off as much as 500 pounds of meat from the body of its prey in one bite.

By studying fossils of *T. rex* skulls, scientists have made some interesting discoveries. They found out that *T. rex* had excellent hearing and vision, and a keen sense of smell. These senses, combined with strong legs made for running and a 4-foot-long skull, made it a deadly hunter. *T. rex* could sense its prey from a distance, chase it down if it had to, and kill it with one swift chomp.

But hunting takes a lot of energy. It can wear an animal down, especially if the hunt doesn't succeed. So scientists think that *T. rex* also ate the bodies of animals they found that were already dead. Lions and other large predators today eat both animals they kill and carcasses (bodies of dead animals) they find. It makes sense to assume that *T. rex* did the same. When a 40-ton sauropod—or even a 3-ton duck-billed dinosaur—died in the forest, *something* had to eat all that meat.

CARCHARODONTOSAURUS

(kar-CHAR-uh-DON-tuh-SAW-rus)

Carcharodontosaurus was even larger than *Tyrannosaurus*. The entire animal was a good 45 feet long from its nose to the end of its tail. Its massive skull was a whopping 5 ½ feet long, nearly a foot larger than that of *Tyrannosaurus*. But while it may have had a larger head than *Tyrannosaurus*, scientists think it may not have been as smart. Its brain was only half as large as that of a *T. rex*.

Like the *T. rex*, *Carcharodontosaurus* was a theropod dinosaur. That makes them distant cousins, even though they lived 20 million years and thousands of miles apart. They both had short arms and probably attacked with their huge mouths full of biting teeth. But the teeth of *Tyrannosaurus* were thick, like rail-

road spikes. The teeth of *Carcharodontosaurus* were thinner, like steak knives. In some ways, this deadly dinosaur's teeth are like those of the great white shark. That's why it was named *Carcharodontosaurus*, which means "great-white-shark-toothed lizard."

Carcharodontosaurus is the largest meat-eating dinosaur ever found in Africa. It lived about 90 million years ago, which makes it a more ancient animal than *Tyrannosaurus rex*.

A pair of *Carcharodontosaurus* attack a sauropod they have separated from its herd.

Carcharodontosaurus defends a carcass from another theropod hunter/scavenger, *Deltadromeus.*

GIGANOTOSAURUS

(Gi-GAN-uh-toe-SAW-rus)

Giganotosaurus was an even more ancient and probably larger theropod than *Carcharodontosaurus*. In fact, at 45 to 50 feet long and 8 tons of weight, it is the heaviest and longest meat-eating dinosaur ever discovered. Some scientists think that these two dinosaurs belonged to the same family of theropods, but more study is needed to confirm this.

Giganotosaurus lived about 100 million years ago in South America. With teeth 8 inches long, it could probably bite through even the toughest of hides. But it probably wasn't a very fast runner. An animal as large and heavy as *Giganotosaurus* usually doesn't find its prey by outrunning it. That would be like an elephant chasing down a gazelle or a cheetah—not very likely. Scientists think that *Giganotosaurus* ate animals that had already died, or killed and ate animals that were crippled and about to die.

Although *Giganotosaurus* looks much like *Tyrannosaurus rex,* the two were not related. During the time period that *Giganotosaurus* was alive, North America and South America were not connected. So *Giganotosaurus* could not have traveled to North America to become the ancestor of *T. rex,* which lived millions of years later. Also, even though they were both giant meat eaters, the skeletal features of the two dinosaurs are quite different. This tells scientists that they must have belonged to different families.

**Giganotosaurus (left and below) is the largest
meat-eating dinosaur ever discovered. It probably
scavenged on dead and dying animals.**

A pair of *Giganotosaurus* get lucky. They have found
a crippled *Amargasaurus*, lagging behind its herd.
The sail-backed plant eater doesn't stand a chance.

The Deadliest Dinosaurs

ALLOSAURUS

(al-uh-SAW-rus)

Allosaurus, with its massive head filled with steak-knife sharp teeth, was a fearsome hunter. It was also huge, growing up to 30 feet or more in length, and weighing at least 2 tons. This deadly theropod had long legs and powerful arms, with hands that ended in three sharply clawed fingers. It also had bony ridges above and in front of its eyes, giving it the appearance of having horns when seen straight on.

Allosaurus lived at the same time as the giant sauropods of North America and probably hunted them. A single *Allosaurus* might have been able to bring down a baby sauropod, but not a full-grown adult (unless it was sick and couldn't defend itself). Perhaps *Allosaurus* hunted in packs, like modern wolves, when attacking the 60-to-100-foot-long giants.

Allosaurus may have been good parents to their young. Evidence from a recently discovered *Allosaurus* nest suggests they brought pieces of freshly killed sauropods back to the nest for their babies to nibble on.

Allosaurus fossils have been found in North and South America, Africa, Asia, and Australia, indicating it was a very successful animal. It lived from 155 to 145 million years ago. Its name means "different lizard." This refers to the differences between it and *Megalosaurus* (MEG-uh-low-SAW-rus), which was the very first theropod dinosaur to be discovered and named.

Opposite: *Allosaurus* was big and fast. It could take down a smaller dinosaur by itself. Below: A pack of *Allosaurus* tries to get a baby *Brachiosaurus* away from its mother.

DEINONYCHUS

(die-NON-ih-kus)

Deinonychus may not have been the biggest dinosaur, but it certainly was one of the most dangerous. Built for hunting and killing, this small theropod had long, powerful legs with which to run down its prey. It had a long, narrow tail, which it held out stiffly behind it for balance. Many bony rods ran down the length of the tail to help keep it straight. *Deinonychus* had long arms and slender hands with three fingers, each of which ended in a long, sharp claw. It had a large head and a long snout filled with razor-sharp teeth.

But this killing machine had deadlier weapons than its speed and nasty teeth. The second toe on each foot was not used for walking—it was a weapon. It was turned upward and bore a 6-inch-long, sharply curved claw. *Deinonychus,* in fact, means "terrible claw."

Deinonychus could run down its prey and grab hold with its strong arms and claws. Then it could leap upon the animal and tear it apart with swift strokes of its terrifying toe claws. *Deinonychus* was a member of the dromaeosaurid (dro-MAY-uh-SAW-rid) dinosaur family. That means "swift lizard." Small for a theropod, it grew only 10 to 15 feet long and weighed no more than 200 to 250 pounds. It lived about 115 to 110 million years ago in the western United States.

Above and left: The deadly claws of ***Deinonychus*** **made it a hunter to be feared. Inset: These swift, agile dinosaurs were extremely bird-like. One artist has even given the beast a feathery covering.**

VELOCIRAPTOR

(veh-LOS-ih-RAP-tor)

Brains, speed, saw-edged teeth and slashing toe claws made *Velociraptor* a particularly deadly hunter. Like its close cousin, *Deinonychus*, *Velociraptor* was also a member of the dromaeo-saurid dinosaur family. *Velociraptor* means "swift plunderer" or "robber."

Velociraptor was not a large theropod, reaching only about 6 feet in length. But it was a fast-moving, lethal predator. It had a long, thin tail held stiffly behind it for balance, like *Deinonychus*. And it had long arms and long hands ending in sharp, grasping claws. It could capture its prey with its clawed hands, then slash it to death with its long, curved toe claws.

Velociraptor had a long, low head that held a surprisingly large brain, and a lengthy snout filled with sharp teeth made to bite through flesh. Its jaws were hinged like those of a snake. This allowed it to open its mouth very wide and bite off huge chunks of meat at a time.

Velociraptor lived about 85 to 80 million years ago in Asia and eastern Europe.

Below: Another bird-like theropod, this *Velociraptor* (losing a battle to a *Protoceratops*) is pictured with downy feathers. Opposite: A pair of *Velociraptor* in a nest they've made of leaves and branches. Opposite, bottom: *Velociraptor* was small, fast, and probably hunted in packs.

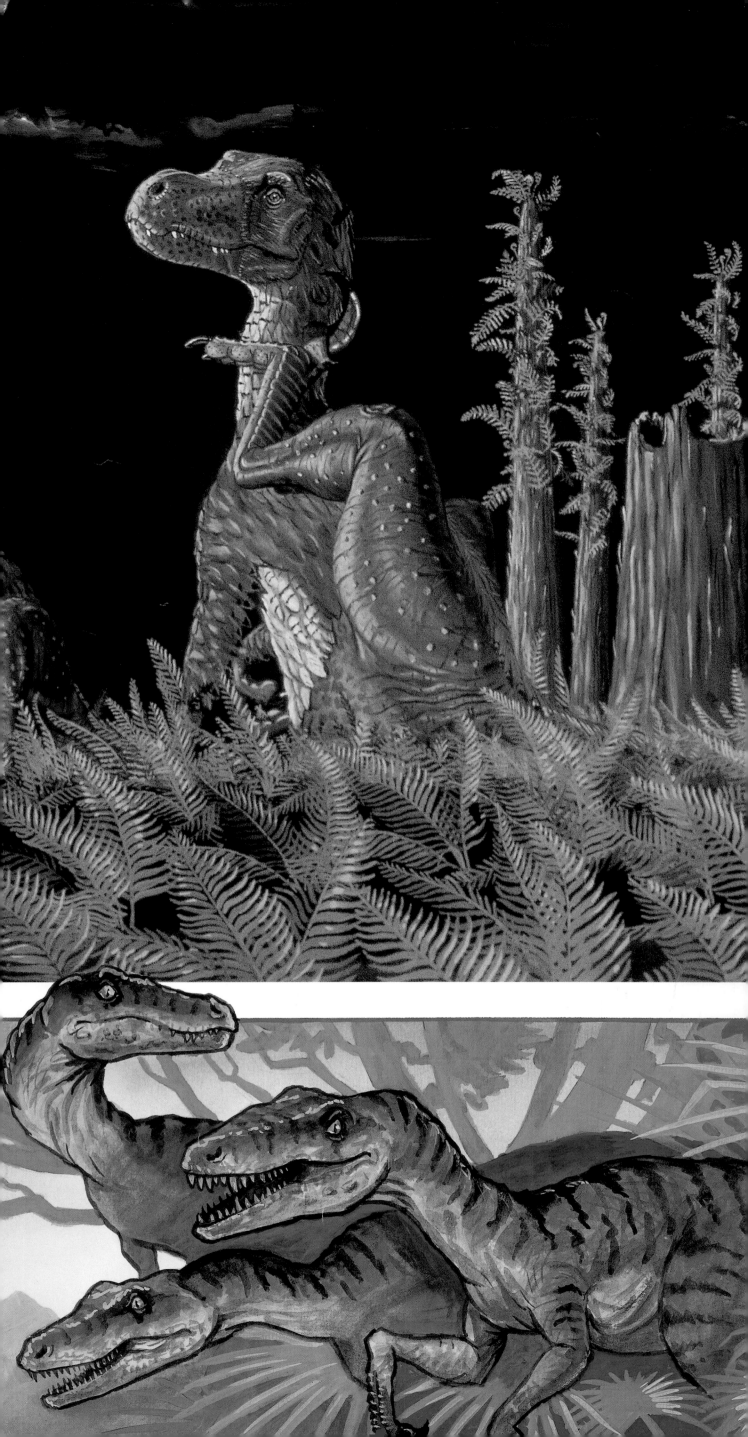

UTAHRAPTOR

(YOO-tah-RAP-tor)

Utahraptor may have been the deadliest dinosaur hunter that ever lived. It was a medium-sized theropod, growing to about 20 feet in length. Like *Deinonychus*, it was a member of the dromaeosaurid dinosaur family. It, too, had a large brain, good eyesight, and a curved claw on the third toe of each of its feet. But these razor-edged weapons put those of *Deinonychus* to shame. *Utahraptor*'s upturned toe claws grew to be 12 inches long—twice the size of *Deinonychus*'s.

A two-legged meat eater, *Utahraptor* could run down its prey on its long, strong legs. It could rip open the belly of its victims with one quick slash of its sickle-shaped toe claws.

Scientists think that *Utahraptor* may have hunted in packs, like other dromaeosaurids. They could have attacked and killed a giant sauropod by working together, like a pride of lions stalking a water buffalo.

Utahraptor lived in the western United States about 125 million years ago. Its name means "Utah plunderer" or "Utah robber," which refers to the place where it was discovered.

Inset: A pack of *Utahraptors* attack an iguanodontid dinosaur. Below: A pair of the deadly dinosaurs on the prowl for prey.

The Strangest-Looking Dinosaurs

AMARGASAURUS

(uh-MAR-guh-SAW-rus)

Amargasaurus was a sauropod dinosaur that lived in South America around 130 to 125 million years ago. It wasn't a giant sauropod, like *Brachiosaurus* or *Seismosaurus*. In fact, for a sauropod it was rather small, only about 30 feet long— the size of a big elephant. But it was the strangest-looking plant eater ever discovered.

Amargasaurus had two rows of long spines sticking up from its backbone. The spines ran down its neck, along its back, and down its tail. In life, the spines

would have been covered with skin, creating a sail on the dinosaur's back. However, scientists can't tell if the spines supported one thick sail or two thinner, parallel ones.

Some scientists think the spines served to protect *Amargasaurus*. They would have made it hard for a large predator like *Megalosaurus* to chomp down on *Amargasaurus*'s neck. The long sail of skin stretched over the spines would also have helped keep this dinosaur cool. Other dinosaurs that lived near the equator had similar spines to support sails on their backs. Another reason for having such a large sail could have been to signal other dinosaurs of its kind. If the sail had colorful patterns, it may have been used to attract a mate.

Amargasaurus means "lizard of La Amarga," which refers to the place in Argentina where it was found.

Amargasaurus is pictured here with its sail extending from the back of the neck to the base of the tail. The artist has chosen to expose the two rows of spines from behind the head to halfway down the neck. But no one knows exactly how the spines of Amargasaurus were covered by skin.

Parasaurolophus may have had skin coloring for camouflage or to attract a mate. Here are three possible colorations. The skeleton shows the arrangement of the bones that held the tail straight out and back.

PARASAUROLOPHUS

(PAR-uh-SAW-ruh-LOW-fus)

Parasaurolophus was a member of the hadrosaurid (HAD-ruh-SAW-rid) family of duck-billed dinosaurs. It had a spoon-shaped, duck-like beak. But that wasn't its oddest feature. This 30-foot-long plant eater had a 6-foot-long skull crest of curved, hollow bones. This stretched from the front of its nose to behind and above the back of its head. It may have been covered by skin, giving the dinosaur a startling crest from the top of its head back to the base of its neck.

Scientists aren't exactly sure what the tube-like bones were for. But they found air passages leading from the nostrils up through the bony tubes. This means that *Parasaurolophus* could blow air through them, like a trombone. Perhaps these dinosaurs used the hollow bones to amplify their calls to each other. Some scientists think that males used this sound chamber to bellow challenges to their rivals. And the long nasal passages certainly helped to increase the dinosaur's sense of smell.

Parasaurolophus could walk on its hind legs as well as on all fours. When it browsed for food in the forest, it probably moved in four-legged fashion. But it probably ran just on its hind legs.

This duck-billed dinosaur lived in western North America about 75 to 65 million years ago. Its name means "similar crested lizard," which refers to another duck-billed dinosaur, *Saurolophus* (sore-OL-uh-fus). This animal, which was discovered before *Parasaurolophus*, also had a head crest. But its crest was solid rather than hollow, and it was a much smaller dinosaur.

Inset: The amazing hollow skull crest of *Parasaurolophus* is exposed. No one knows for sure if there was a flap of skin from the top of the crest to the base of the neck (as pictured left) or not (as pictured below).

THERIZINOSAURUS

(THER-ih-ZEE-nuh-SAW-rus)

Therizinosaurus may be the strangest-looking animal that ever lived. An entire skeleton has never been found, but the pieces discovered so far are amazing. This two-legged meat eater's name means "scythe lizard," and it was named that for a good reason. It had arms over 8 feet long. And its fingers were tipped with huge, curved claws. One fossil claw discovered was over 2½ feet long!

This long-armed, multi-bladed hunter was a theropod. But a typical theropod, like *Tyrannosaurus* or *Velociraptor*, had a large head with massive jaws and long, sharp teeth made for biting and tearing flesh. *Therizinosaurus* had the long neck and small head of a bird-mimic dinosaur. And its broad-billed beak lacked teeth in the front.

Some scientists suggest that *Therizinosaurus* used its enormous claws to rip into and dig open termite mounds. But this strange beast was about 25 feet long and probably weighed over a ton. It would take a lot of termites to satisfy its appetite. Until more fossils are found, the question of what this dinosaur hunted and what it ate will remain a mystery.

Therizinosaurus lived in Mongolia about 70 to 65 million years ago.

Weird-looking *Therizinosaurus* is given different looks here by different artists. Left: A bird-like neck wattle and head feathers, plus zebra stripes, make this one a showy animal. Above: Somber skin tones and a lack of display features would help this animal blend in rather than stand out.

SIBBICK 95

BARYONYX

(BAR-ee-ON-icks)

This dinosaur was a living nightmare. Imagine a 30-foot-long crocodile with 2-foot-long jaws armed with sharp, jagged-edged teeth. Then imagine it can easily run faster than you on its long, strong legs. And imagine that on the thumb of each of its long, grasping hands is a deadly, curved, foot-long claw. And its other two fingers each have a small, but no less deadly, curved claw. Finally, there's the hint of a crest rising along the top of its toothy muzzle. You've just imagined *Baryonyx*, one of the strangest theropods yet discovered.

The name *Baryonyx* means "heavy claw," referring to the deadly weapons on each hand. But they weren't the only weapons this predator had. *Baryonyx* had a long, low, narrow snout similar to that of a crocodile, and like a crocodile it may have caught and eaten fish. It had many more teeth in its jaws than a typical theropod—teeth that were, again, very much like those of a crocodile. Undigested fish scales have been found in the stomach area of one *Baryonyx* fossil. But this large animal couldn't have lived only on fish, and scientists think it must have hunted small land animals as well.

Baryonyx lived in what is now England about 125 million years ago. It is one of several strange-looking meat eaters known from that time and place.

Baryonyx may have hunted for small animals in shallow water (left), or for fish in lakes and rivers (above).

The Spiky, Armored Dinosaurs

STEGOSAURUS

(STEG-uh-SAW-rus)

Stegosaurus had lethal protection from neck to tail. It bristled with deadly spines and bony plates. In fact, its name means "roofed lizard" which refers to the armor plates on its back. A whole family of armored dinosaurs or "roofed lizards," the stegosaurids, was named after it.

Up to 30 feet long and weighing in at 2 tons, *Stegosaurus* had huge, pointed, bony plates that stuck up from its neck and ran halfway down its tail. The thick tail ended in two pairs of giant spikes that stuck out from the sides. They would have made fearsome weapons. *Stegosaurus* probably defended itself by swishing its tail from side to side. Predators would have kept away from those enormous, bony spikes.

For a long time, scientists weren't sure of just how the bony plates were arranged on *Stegosaurus*'s back. At first, they thought the plates ran down the dinosaur's back in two rows. Then they thought there was only one row of alternating plates—one sitting a little bit more to the right side, followed by one sitting a bit more to the left, and so on. Now we know for sure.

An unusual *Stegosaurus* fossil was recently found in Colorado. All of its plates and spines were in the same position as when the dinosaur was alive. It shows that *Stegosaurus* had 2 rows of alternating plates that stuck straight up in the air.

These heavy dinosaurs moved on all fours, with their small heads close to the ground. *Stegosaurus*'s horny beak was good for biting off plants, but its short, weak teeth couldn't chew anything too tough. It may have had a second stomach to help digest plant fiber. *Stegosaurus* lived in the western United States and China about 160 to 150 million years ago.

Above: An *Allosaurus* tries its luck with *Stegosaurus*. But attacking from the side of this plant eater was no safer than attacking from the rear. Below: A *Ceratosaurus* makes the mistake of attacking a *Stegosaurus*. Although slow-moving, this armored plant eater probably won more battles than it lost.

EUOPLOCEPHALUS

(YOO-oh-pluh-SEF-uh-lus)

Euoplocephalus was as well armored as a modern anti-tank vehicle, but it couldn't move nearly as quickly. It was a slow-moving plant eater whose body armor gave it excellent protection from hungry theropods.

Euoplocephalus means "well-armored head." But this dinosaur was well armored over most of its body. From nose to tail, its back and sides were covered with bony plates. The plates were studded with horny spikes 4 to 6 inches long. And the tail ended in a large, bony club. Even its eyes were protected by armor. Each eyelid was actually a small, round bone that closed like a shutter when the dinosaur was attacked.

This plant eater had four stout legs with hoof-like claws on its feet. Its head was wider than it was long, with a broad snout that ended in a horny beak. Like all ankylosaurids, it had many small teeth for chewing plants and cheek pouches to hold unchewed food.

Euoplocephalus had small eyes and probably found its favorite food through smell rather than sight. It is the best known of the armored dinosaurs because it was the most common ankylosaurid in North America. It grew to about 25 feet long and weighed 2 to 3 tons. It lived in western Canada about 75 to 70 million years ago.

Euoplocephalus (top) may have been the most heavily armored dinosaur from snout to tail club. Edmontonia (bottom) was as big as Euoplocephalus, but it lacked the tail club.

EDMONTONIA

(ed-mon-TONE-ee-uh)

This armored plant eater belongs to the nodosaurid (NO-duh-SAW-rid) dinosaur family. They were the first cousins to the ankylosaurids and looked a lot like them. But their body armor was different—they didn't have horns on their heads behind and below their eyes, and they didn't have a tail club. What they had were rows of thick spikes sticking out sideways along the neck and shoulders. Some nodosaurids had spikes all the way down the sides of their bodies right to the tail.

Edmontonia was about 20 to 25 feet long and weighed about 3 tons. It was a big, spiky, tank-like dinosaur that walked on four bulky legs. Bony armor plates and lots of interlocking smaller bones covered its neck, back, and tail, protecting it from attacking predators. Its shoulder spines were particularly large and strong, and would have made a hungry tyrannosaurid think twice.

Edmontonia was named after the Edmonton Formation in Alberta, Canada, where its fossils have been found. It lived about 75 to 70 million years ago in western North America.

TALARURUS

(TAL-uh-ROOR-us)

When *Talarurus* was first discovered in 1952, it was thought to be one of the oldest of the ankylosaurids. The initial reconstruction of this dinosaur made it look like an ancient reptile. The legs sprawled out from the sides and the tail dragged on the ground, making it look like a fat crocodile. More information and new ideas about ankylosaurids led to a new vision of this dinosaur in 1979.

Although it has some ancient features, *Talarurus* is now known to be a late anky-losaurid. It was about 15 feet long, with small teeth and a big belly for digesting plants. Its body was barrel shaped, and it had short, stout legs. Picture a hip-popotamus with body armor and a small horned head—that's probably close to what *Talarurus* looked like.

The name *Talarurus* means "basket tail." This refers to the way the bones at the end of the tail are woven together for stiffness to support the tail club. It lived in the late Cretaceous, about 90 million years ago, in Mongolia.

Talarurus looks like a cross between *Euoplocephalus* and *Edmontonia*. Here it defends itself from a tyrannosaurid dinosaur.

The Fastest, Smartest Dinosaurs

TROODON

(TROH-oh-don)

This little two-legged meat eater had a larger brain, given its body size, than any other dinosaur. It had large eyes and keen vision and was a swift runner.

The size of this dinosaur's brain would have made it as smart as many birds living today, such as ostriches and eagles. Like a bird of prey, *Troodon* would have used its smarts to figure out where and how to catch its favorite food, which was smaller, good at hiding, and possibly faster. *Troodon* had many skeletal features similar to birds. Some scientists think that birds may have come from dinosaurs like the *Troodon*.

Troodon means "wounding tooth." This refers to the shape of its jagged-edged teeth, which were made to slice through flesh. *Troodon* was a small theropod, only reaching a length of about 6 to 8 feet. Two of its toes had claws that were curved and extended, similar to those of *Deinonychus*, but not nearly as long or as lethal. *Troodon* had long arms with sharp-clawed, grasping hands. It lived about 75 to 70 million years ago in western North America.

Right and below: *Troodon* was an extremely bird-like dinosaur. It was agile, swift-moving, had large eyes and good vision.

STRUTHIOMIMUS

(STROOTH-ee-oh-MY-mus)

Struthiomimus was a large, swift member of the ornithomimid (or-NITH-oh-MY-mid), or "bird mimic," dinosaur family. It was a little larger and had stronger arms and hands than the other ornithiomimids. Its fingers ended in powerful, curved claws. Its long legs would have made *Struthiomimus* a fast runner. It had large eyes and, we assume, keen eyesight.

Put it all together, and you get a dinosaur that was probably a successful hunter of whatever it chose to eat. Scientists think ornithomimids ate a variety of foods, from fruits and seeds to lizards and small mammals. Some think they used their long fingers and claws to dig for buried dinosaur eggs. Others think they dug up clams and other shellfish. Fossils of *Struthiomimus* have been found along ancient river banks in northeastern North America.

Struthiomimus, which means "ostrich mimic," had the long, stiff tail and toothless beak typical of all bird-mimic dinosaurs. It grew to a length of about 12 feet, and its brain was large in relation to its body. So *Struthiomimus* was not only faster but probably smarter than the tyrannosaurs and sickle-clawed theropods that hunted it.

Struthiomimus lived about 85 to 80 million years ago.

Struthiomimus was a smart and speedy ornithomimid dinosaur. It could run faster than a race horse.

The First Dinosaurs

EORAPTOR

(EE-oh-RAP-tor)

Eoraptor was an ancient two-legged, meat-eating dinosaur. It lived in South America about 230 to 225 million years ago. Some scientists think it was the most primitive member of the theropods, the dinosaur family that includes the giant meat eaters like *Tyrannosaurus*.

Eoraptor's name means "dawn plunderer." The word "dawn" refers to the beginning of the time of the dinosaurs, not the time just after sunrise. The word "raptor," which means "plunderer," is also used to describe birds of prey, like eagles and hawks.

This early predator was small, only about 3 feet long. Its legs were twice as long as its arms and are the legs of a fast-running animal. Its hands had five fingers, which only the most primitive dinosaurs had.

Eoraptor had two kinds of teeth. Its back teeth were jagged and curved, like those of a meat-eating dinosaur. But its front teeth were broad and leaf-shaped, like those of a plant eater. *Eoraptor* may have been the only dinosaur to have had both kinds of teeth.

Eoraptor is one of the earliest dinosaurs. It lived well before the giant theropods and sauropods. Those animals became specialized to eat only meat or only plants, but tiny Eoraptor apparently could eat both.

STAURIKOSAURUS

(staw-RIK-uh-SAW-rus)

This primitive meat eater is one of the most ancient of all the dinosaurs. It lived in South America about 230 to 225 million years ago. Its name means "cross lizard." This is a reference to the Southern Cross, a constellation of stars visible from South America.

Staurikosaurus was about 7 feet long, was lightly built and weighed only about 70 pounds. It had the long legs and long thin tail of a swift runner. Its arms were short and probably had five-fingered hands. It had a large head and strong jaws filled with sharp teeth.

Staurikosaurus was so ancient it had features of both sauropods and theropods. Scientists think it is most closely related to the theropods and was a member of the herrerasaurid family.

Staurikosaurus is shown here with the coloration of a lizard, which is great camouflage for any forest-dwelling animal.

The Last Dinosaurs

PACHYCEPHALOSAURUS

(PACK-ee-SEF-uh-low-SAW-rus)

Pachycephalosaurus means "thick-headed lizard." This two-legged plant eater is well named. The bone on the top of its skull was 10 inches thick. *Pachycephalosaurus* lived in western North America about 68 to 65 million years ago. It was one of the very last living dinosaurs.

This dinosaur had a whole family named for it, the pachycephalosaurids. They had keen eyesight and a good sense of smell. They walked with their backs parallel to the ground. They held their tails straight back and high for balance. They came in all sizes, from very small to the size of a truck. And they all had that enormously thick skull.

Pachycephalosaurus is the largest of the so-called "boneheads." It grew to about 15 feet long. It had sharp knobs and bony spikes above its nose and on the back of its head.

Some scientists think the thick skulls were used in head-butting contests. Bighorn sheep and other animals do that today, to see which is the strongest.

TRICERATOPS

(try-SER-uh-tops)

Triceratops was a member of the ceratopsid (ser-uh-TOP-sid) dinosaur family. These horned dinosaurs had a wide variety of bony frills and horns on their heads and necks. *Triceratops* means "three-horned-face."

Two long, solid horns rose from above Triceratops' eyes. The third horn grew from the snout, just above the nose. The two eye horns grew quite large, perhaps as much as 5 feet long. This four-legged plant eater weighed up to 6 tons and grew to a length of 30 feet.

Triceratops had a broad, massive head frill that grew out from the back of its skull. The frill would have made it difficult for an attacking dinosaur to grab it by its neck. Its head and frill formed nearly one third of its entire length.

Triceratops had a bony beak and teeth made for biting through plants and slicing them up. It may have eaten ferns and other plants with soft leaves. As its sharp cropping teeth wore down and fell out, new ones were already there to replace them. This dinosaur's strong jaws gave it the most powerful bite of any plant eater in the animal kingdom. And the sharp, parrot-like beak would have made a good defensive weapon.

Probably the last living ceratopsid dinosaur, *Triceratops* lived all over western North America about 70 to 65 million years ago.

Left: *Triceratops* moved in large herds across the land, eating tons of plants as they moved. Here the artist shows two males fighting for the right to lead the herd. Top: A similar battle to see which is strongest takes place between two *Pachycephalosaurus*.

The Earliest Discoveries

HYLAEOSAURUS

(hi-LAY-uh-SAW-rus)

Hylaeosaurus was the first armored dinosaur ever discovered and the third dinosaur to be given a scientific name. It was a four-legged plant eater that lived in England about 140 to 130 million years ago, along with *Iguanodon*. *Hylaeosaurus* had bony armor covering its back, and spikes sticking out along its sides and tail. Its armor was made of bony knobs with a horny covering over the skin. These knobs grew together, or fused, into a solid shield over the hips. This bulky beast grew to about 15 to 20 feet long.

Hylaeosaurus was a member of the nodosaurid family of armored dinosaurs. Its name means "forest lizard," which refers to the Wealden Formation, in England, where the fossil was found. ("Weald" is an old English word for "forest.") The first *Hylaeosaurus* fossil was discovered in 1832.

This stout dinosaur had a long, narrow head. It probably fed on ground plants and insects. Its armor plating and spikes made *Hylaeosaurus* a fearsome creature. Meat-eating dinosaurs could outrun it, but they would have had a difficult time sinking their teeth into the spikes and armor plating that covered *Hylaeosaurus*.

Above: *Hylaeosaurus* **is attacked by a pack of theropods.
It will probably lose the fight, but at least one of its
attackers will suffer terrible wounds. Opposite:** *Iguanodon*
**is shown moving on both two legs and all fours.
Inset: An** *Iguanodon* **uses its thumb spike to defend itself.**

IGUANODON

(ih-GWAN-oh-don)

Iguanodon was the second ancient animal to be identified as a dinosaur. (The first was *Megalosaurus,* a primitive theropod discovered in England and described scientifically in the 1820s.) *Iguanodon* was a large plant eater, but not one of the giants. It was about 25 to 35 feet long and could weigh up to 5 tons. When it stood on its hind limbs, its head could reach branches 16 to 18 feet high. A whole family of plant eaters, called the iguanodontids, was named after it.

Because it had stout hind limbs and shorter, thinner front ones, scientists think *Iguanodon* probably moved on all fours when walking. But it probably ran on its two hind legs, and very likely could move quite fast when it had to.

Iguanodon is famous for the large, spiky thumbs on its hands. They may have been used in defense or to help the dinosaur gather food. *Iguanodon* fossils have been found all around the world. The first was discovered in a rock quarry in England in 1818 and given to Gideon Mantell. He was a doctor who lived nearby and was known to collect interesting fossils. But it would be another 60 years before complete *Iguanodon* fossils were discovered. Until then, it was thought that *Iguanodon* was some kind of giant four-legged lizard with a spike on its nose. (That's because only one thumb spike was found with the first fossil.)

Iguanodon lived about 140 to 130 million years ago. Its name means "iguana tooth," because its teeth are similar to those of the iguana lizard.

The Recent Discoveries

CRYOLOPHOSAURUS

(Cry-uh-LOFF-uh-SAW-rus)

Cryolophosaurus was first discovered in 1991 in Antarctica, the frozen continent on the bottom of the world. It is the first meat-eating dinosaur discovered there. When dinosaurs lived in Antarctica, the continent was much warmer than it is today and not as far to the south.

Cryolophosaurus was a medium-to-large-sized theropod, about 15 to 25 feet long. It had a large head and a jaw filled with teeth designed to cut through flesh. It also had a strange, wavy, bony crest on the top of its head. It reminded the scientists who first studied *Cryolophosaurus* of the 1950s rock-and-roller Elvis Presley. They thought the crest looked like Elvis's hair, and almost named this dinosaur *Elvisaurus*.

Cryolophosaurus, which means "icy crested lizard," lived in Antarctica about 175 million years ago.

Above: *Cryolophosaurus*, the first theropod discovered in Antarctica, is pictured here with its Elvis-like crest. **Inset:** A group of *Cryolophosaurus* stops at the edge of a clearing to scan for prey.

SUCHOMIMUS

(SOOK-uh-MIME-us)

In 1997, an amazing theropod dinosaur was discovered in western Africa. It is called *Suchomimus*, and it was a close cousin to *Baryonyx*, only larger. *Suchomimus* had a longer, narrower head than *Baryonyx*, more teeth (perhaps as many as 100), and a tall ridge or short sail along its back. As with *Baryonyx, Suchomimus* had a huge claw and two smaller ones on each hand. The major claws were over a foot long.

Scientists think that *Suchomimus* hunted and ate fish. That's because its snout was shaped like those of fish-eating crocodiles, and its teeth were quite similar as well. Like today's fish-eating crocodiles, *Suchomimus* had a cluster of special teeth right at the front of its snout with which it could hold onto its slippery prey. It makes sense that this dinosaur's name means "crocodile mimic."

Suchomimus lived in Africa around the same time as *Carcharodontosaurus* and *Deltadromeus*, about 100 million years ago.

Suchomimus had competition for fish from real crocodiles, like this 50-foot-long Sarcosuchus, which was an even more imposing predator than the dinosaur it is attacking.

DINOSAURS SITES TO VISIT ON THE WORLD WIDE WEB

Is there a computer in your home? Is there one at your school or in a public library that you can use? If so, your dinosaur adventures are just beginning. Listed below are dinosaur sites on the World Wide Web that you can visit through your computer. Each one is different. Each offers new information and its own special tour through the world of the giant beasts. You'll meet other fans of dinosaurs through these sites, as well as dinosaur artists and scientists. You'll find dinosaur-related activities, and fun dino stuff to buy as well. And you can find many, many more amazing dinosaur Web sites by going to the Paleo Ring, through which you can visit hundreds of sites around the world.

DINODON
http://www.dinodon.com

DINOSAURIA ON LINE
http://www.dinosauria.com

MASTER DINOSAUR LIST
http://www.crl.com/~sarima/dinosaurs/genera

THE NATURAL HISTORY MUSEUM, LONDON
http://www.nhm.ac.uk/

PALEO RING
http://www.pitt.edu/~mattf/PaleoRing.html

THE ROYAL TYRRELL MUSEUM, DRUMHELLER, ALBERTA, CANADA
http://tyrrell.magtech.ab.ca/

THE SMITHSONIAN INSTITUTION
http://nmnh.si.edu/departments/paleo.html

UNIVERSITY OF CALIFORNIA MUSEUM OF PALEONTOLOGY
http://www.ucmp.berkeley.edu/index.html

Above: A herd of *Triceratops* forms a protective circle around their young as a pair of *Tyrannosaurus* look for an opening to attack.

THE MAJOR DINOSAUR GROUPS

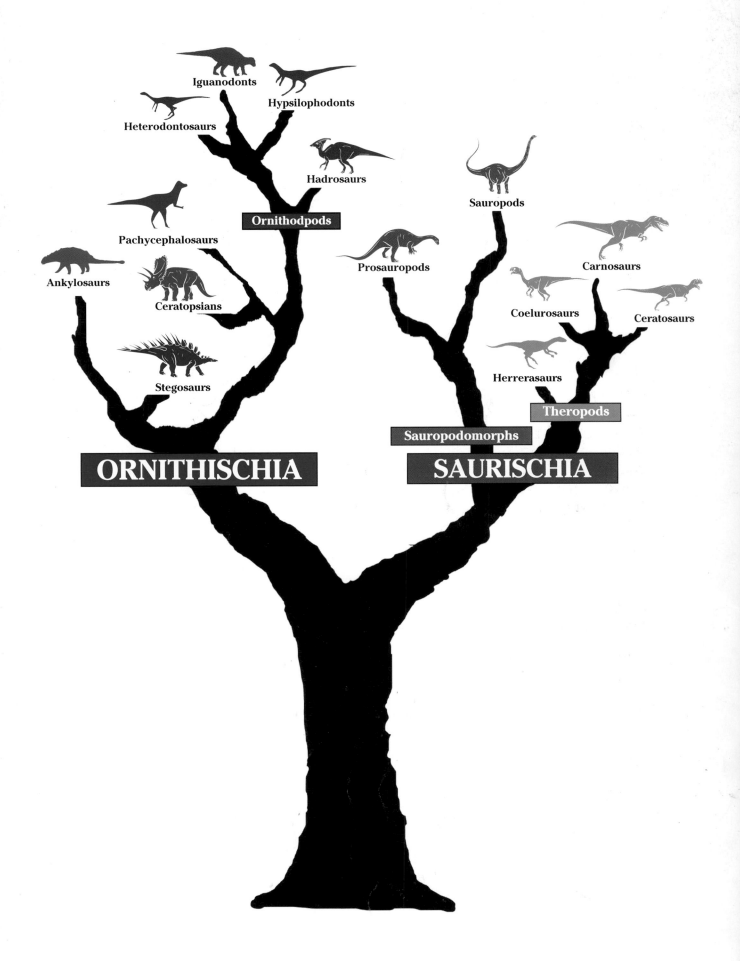

Iguanodonts

Hypsilophodonts

Heterodontosaurs

Hadrosaurs

Sauropods

Pachycephalosaurs

Ornithodpods

Carnosaurs

Ankylosaurs

Prosauropods

Coelurosaurs

Ceratosaurs

Ceratopsians

Herrerasaurs

Stegosaurs

Theropods

Sauropodomorphs

ORNITHISCHIA

SAURISCHIA

DINOSAUR GROUP PORTRAITS

Theropods

Stegosaurids

Ankylosaurids

Prosauropods

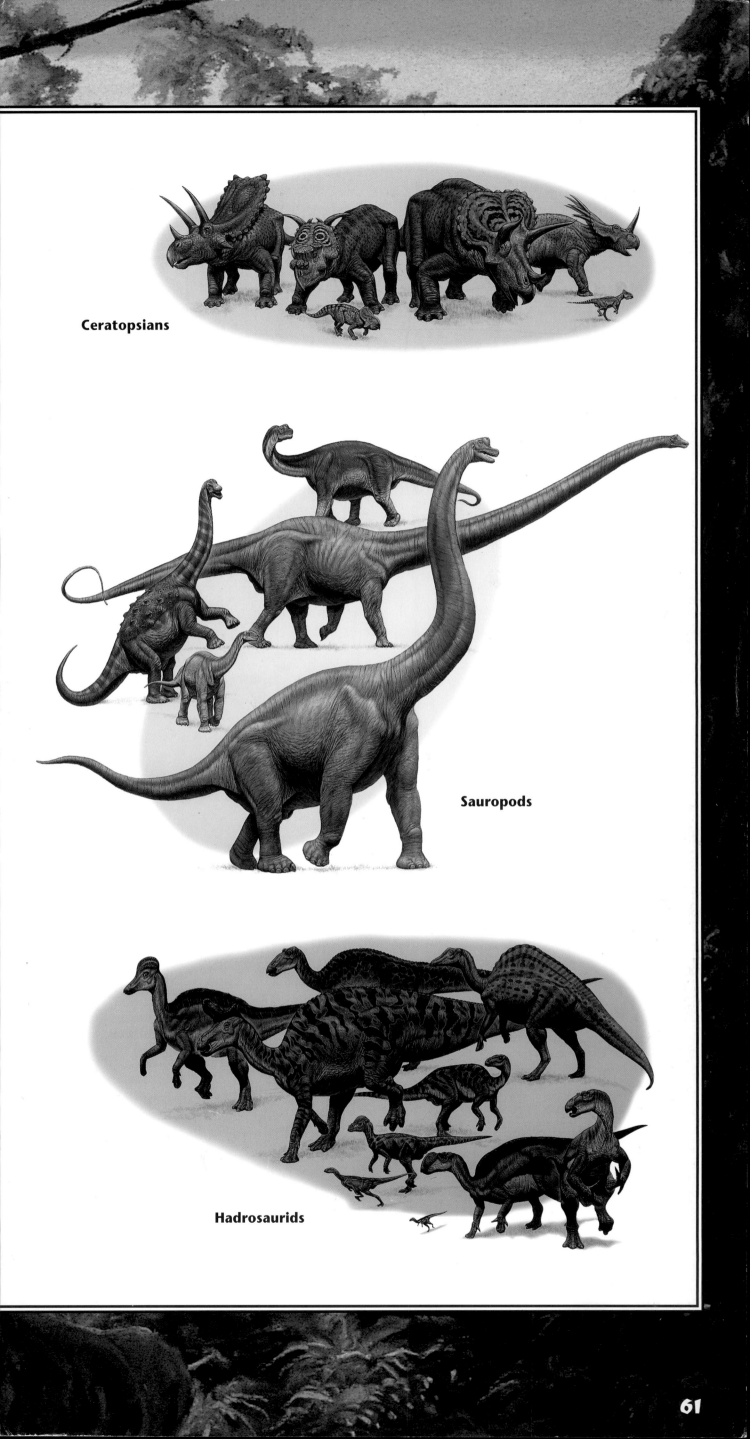

Ceratopsians

Sauropods

Hadrosaurids

INDEX

ART CREDITS